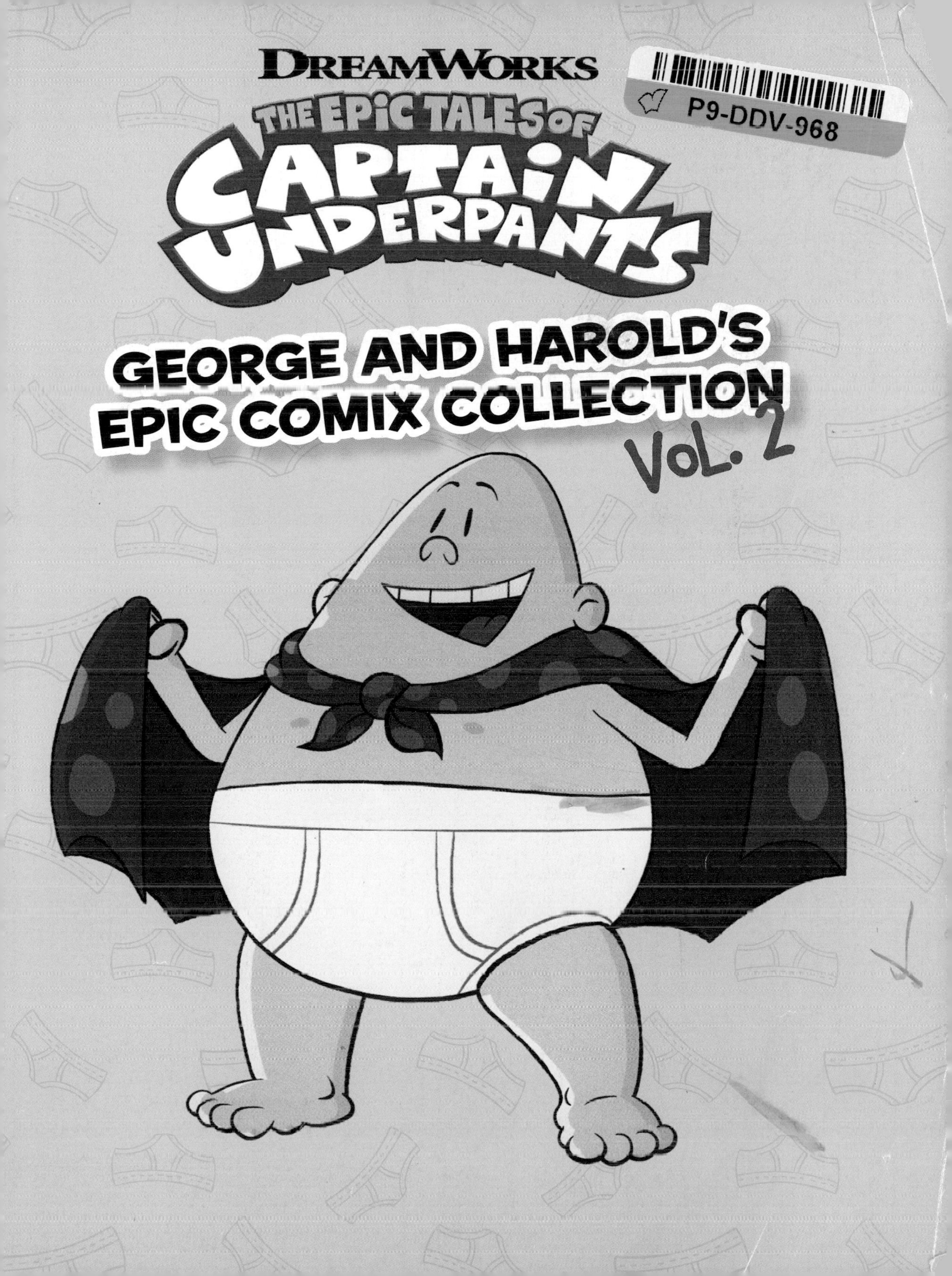
DreamWorks
THE EPIC TALES OF
CAPTAIN UNDERPANTS
GEORGE AND HAROLD'S
EPIC COMIX COLLECTION
VOL. 2

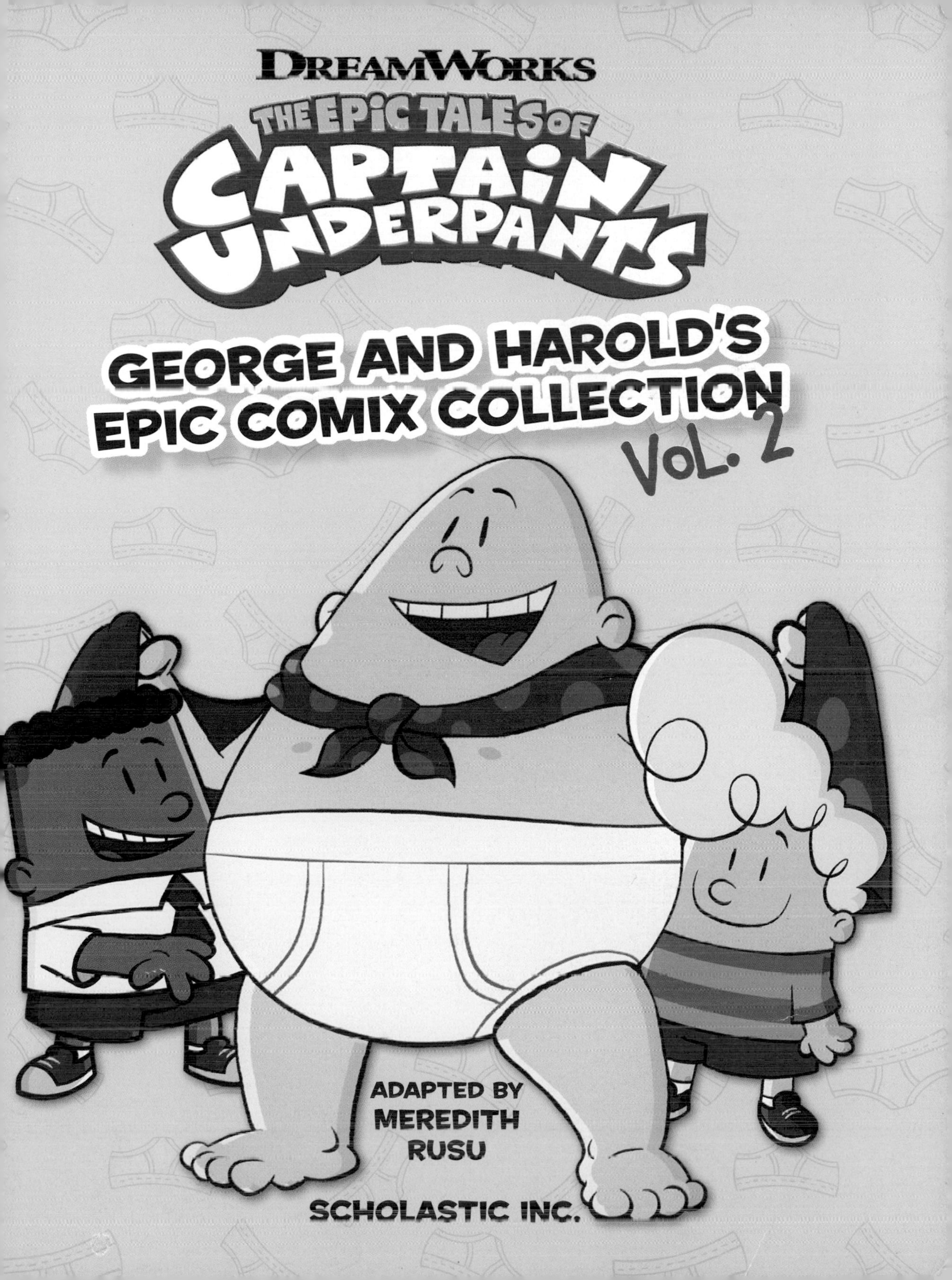
DREAMWORKS
THE EPIC TALES OF
CAPTAIN UNDERPANTS
GEORGE AND HAROLD'S
EPIC COMIX COLLECTION
VOL. 2
ADAPTED BY
MEREDITH
RUSU
SCHOLASTIC INC.

Photos ©: 38-39 background and throughout: vectorplus/Shutterstock.

ISBN 978-1-338-26247-6

10 9 8 7 6 5 21 22 23 24

Printed in the U.S.A. 40

First printing 2020

Book design by Erin McMahon

CONTENTS

Tree House Comix, Inc. Presents:
An Even More Epic Collection of Captain Underpants Comics!

THIS IS GEORGE BEARD AND HAROLD HUTCHINS. GEORGE IS THE KID ON THE LEFT WITH A FLAT TOP AND WORKPLACE-APPROVED SHIRT. HAROLD IS THE ONE ON THE RIGHT WITH THE BAD HAIRCUT AND THE LOOK OF ~~CONSTIPATION~~ CONCENTRATION. REMEMBER THAT NOW.

TOGETHER, GEORGE AND HAROLD MAKE COMIC BOOKS ABOUT THEIR FAVORITE SUPERHERO, CAPTAIN UNDERPANTS. GEORGE WRITES THEM, AND HAROLD ILLUSTRATES THEM. THERE ARE LITERALLY THOUSANDS OF COMIC PAGES LYING AROUND THEIR BEDROOMS. SERIOUSLY, THOUSANDS.

GEORGE AND HAROLD ONCE PUT TOGETHER AN EPIC COLLECTION OF THEIR FAVORITE CAPTAIN UNDERPANTS COMICS. BUT THEN THEY THOUGHT, WOULDN'T IT BE EVEN *MORE* EPIC TO PUT TOGETHER *ANOTHER* VOLUME? AN EVEN BETTER ONE, WITH BIGGER BATTLES, WEDGIER WEDGIES, POOPIER POOP MONSTERS, MASSIVE M.I.S.F.A.R.T. MAYHEM, AND DEEPER VILLAIN BACKSTORIES THAT HOLD A MIRROR UP TO SOCIETY? THE ANSWER, OF COURSE, WAS **UH, YEAH!**

WHAT HAPPENED AFTER THAT IS THE BOOK YOU HOLD IN YOUR HANDS: *GEORGE AND HAROLD'S EPIC COMIX COLLECTION: VOL. 2.* THE STORIES IN THIS VOLUME ARE ILLUSTRATIVE MASTERPIECES, THE CROWN JEWELS OF TREE HOUSE COMIX, INC. (AT LEAST UNTIL GEORGE AND HAROLD CREATE EVEN BETTER ONES.) SO, WHAT ARE YOU WAITING FOR? SLAP ON YOUR FAVORITE PAIR OF TIGHTY-WHITIES (OR BOXER BRIEFS, IF YOU'RE INTO THAT), **Tra-La-Turn the page, and let's get going!**

CAPTAIN UNDERPANTS
AND THE DREADFUL DEBACLE
of DJ DROWSY DRAWERS
DJ DROWSY

Once upon a time, our school was gonna have a dance.
All the kids were excited because they loved dancing.
YAY!!
SCHOOL DANCE SOON!
DANCE
HERE
NOT HERE
YAY!
YAY!
But the mean principal hated dancing.
BORING PRINCIPAL
NO SHAKING!
BUTTS ARE FOR SITTING, NOT SHAKING!

I'LL RUIN THE DANCE BY HIRING THE MOST BORING DJ IN THE PHONE BOOK.
He says—
DJ DROWSY DRAWERS? YOU'RE HIRED!
DJ
But it was a trap! DJ Drowsy Drawers was an evil alien robot lady!
BAHAHAA!!*
HAHAA!
DJ
* EVIL LAUGH

At the dance, DJ Drowsy Drawers played boring beats and did boring rap.
SLEEP
BORING MUSIC
MINE
YOU'RE GETTING VERY SLEEPY! MY FLUTES'LL MAKE YOU YAWN AND MY HARPS'LL MAKE YOU SNORE!
The kids tried to dance, but they couldn't stay awake.
YAWN.

Just then, Captain Underpants swooped in.
ZZZZZ
RAFFLE
I HEAR THERE'S A RAFFLE FOR WALKIE-TALKIES!
GULP! GULP!
SODA
And he drank a whole bunch of soda.
12

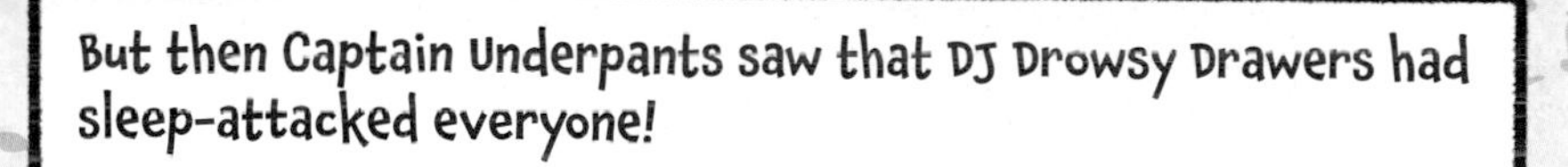
But then Captain Underpants saw that DJ Drowsy Drawers had sleep-attacked everyone!

DJ
ZZZZ
ZZZ
ZZZ
ZZZ
ZZZ
YOU'RE NEXT, UNDYPANTS!
DJ

But Captain Underpants fought back—for truth, justice . . .
TRUTH
JUSTICE
. . . and he kinda wanted those walkie-talkies.

So he stuffed his ears with pre-shrunk cotton.
NOW I CAN'T HEAR YOU! HERE'S YOUR WAKE-UP CALL—IT'S PUNCH O'CLOCK!
DJ
DJ Drowsy Drawers swung back . . .
DJ

. . . and knocked Captain Underpants to the next page—right next to the walkie-talkies.

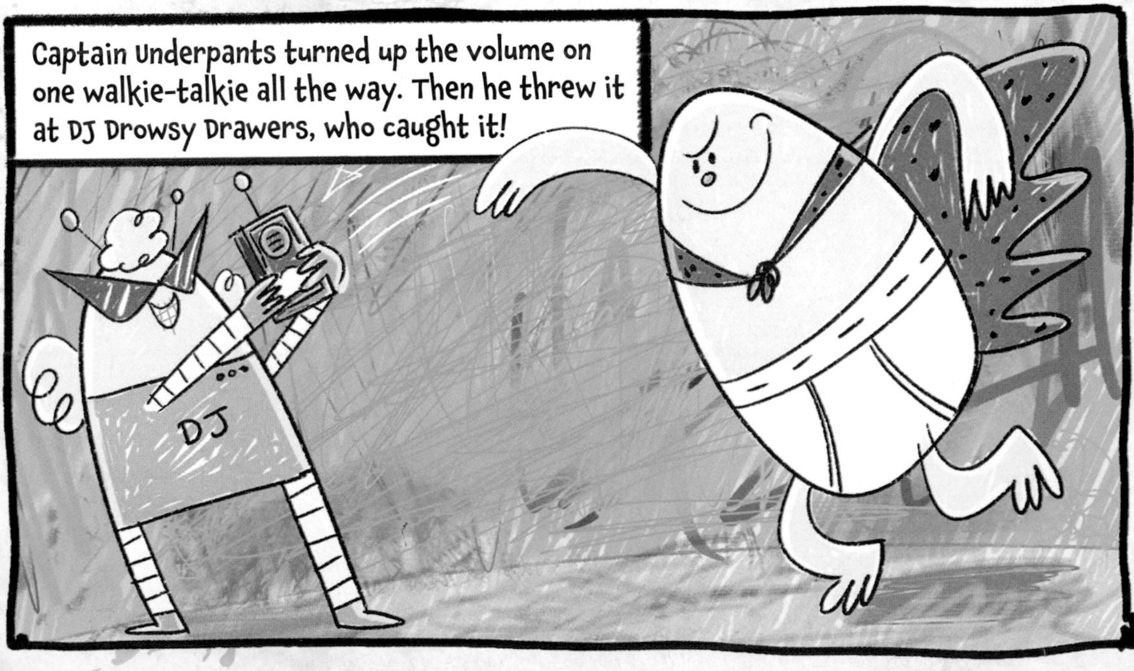

Captain Underpants turned up the volume on one walkie-talkie all the way. Then he threw it at DJ Drowsy Drawers, who caught it!

BAAAAAAAAAAAAA
DJ
Then Captain Underpants took his and burped into it.
It was so loud that all the nuts and bolts popped out of DJ Drowsy Drawers. She fell to the ground in pieces.
DJ
"Hooray!" yelled everyone who was asleep. And then they all learned the Underpants Dance.
SCHOOL DANCE!
TRA-LA-LAAAAA! The end.

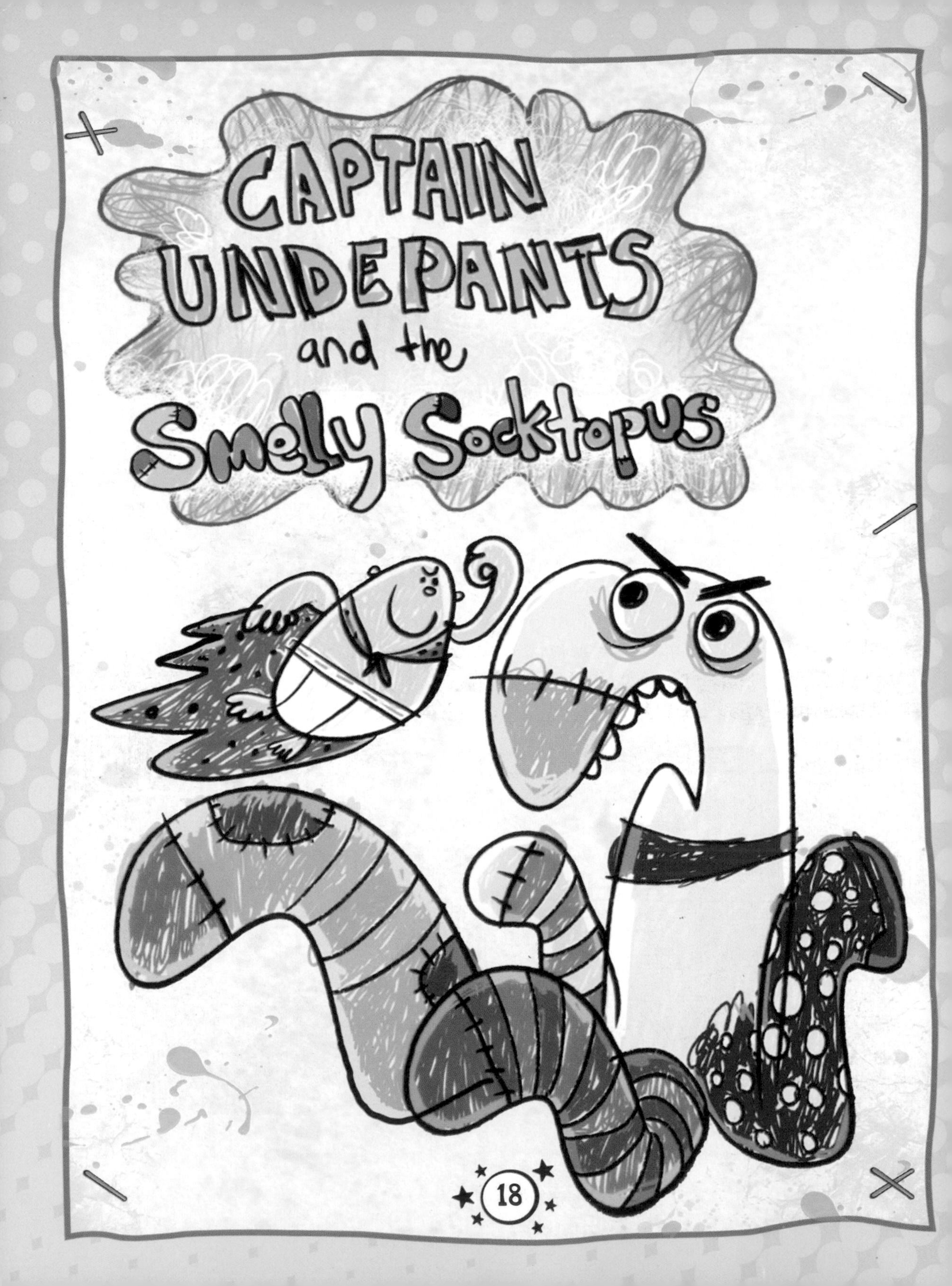
CAPTAIN
UNDEPANTS
and the
Smelly Socktopus

Once there was this alien sock that was super stinky.
His name was Stinky Space Sock, and he was even stinkier than all the feet guys on his home planet, Footsia.
WE'RE OVER IT, SOCK. YOU'RE EXILED AND STUFF! GO STINK UP ANOTHER PLANET.
They gave Stinky Space Sock the big ol' boot. Like, an actual big ol' boot. And they kicked it into space!

Stinky Space Sock landed on Earth, right in a laundry basket full of stinky socks outside George and Harold's gym class. What are the odds?
Stinky Space Sock took one sniff and was all:
I'M HOME!
He tried talking to the other socks, but they didn't talk back because they were sock socks, not living alien socks. But Stinky Space Sock had an idea.
JOIN ME, SMELLY BROTHERS AND SISTERS, AND BECOME ALIVE!

Stinky Space Sock used alien-sock static cling to stick all the other socks to himself . . .
. . . and became the colossal Smelly Socktopus!

I'M MAKING EARTH INTO NEW FOOTSIA! A PLANET THAT'S SO STINKY, IT'S COOL!
NEW FOOTSIA

Smelly Socktopus started swinging its sock tentacles all over town, stinking up everything.
Luckily, Captain Underpants soared in.
TRA-LA-LAAAAA-COUGH! YIKES, WHO'S GRILLING FARTBURGERS?

While Captain Underpants was busy holding his nose, a sock tentacle grabbed him and gave him a squeeze as strong as its stench.

But Captain Underpants thought fast and escaped!
WAISTBAND WIGGLE!

MINI-GOLF!
Captain Underpants led Socktopus to a mini-golf course . . .
GOLF!
LAST HOLE!
. . . trapped the monster in the giant shoe on the last hole . . .

. . . and used his waistband to Stretchy Slingshot the whole big, giant shoe full of Socktopus back into space!
Stinky Space JAiL
And to this day, Smelly Socktopus remains imprisoned in the Shoe Quadrant with the other rejected space shoes. Forever. The end.

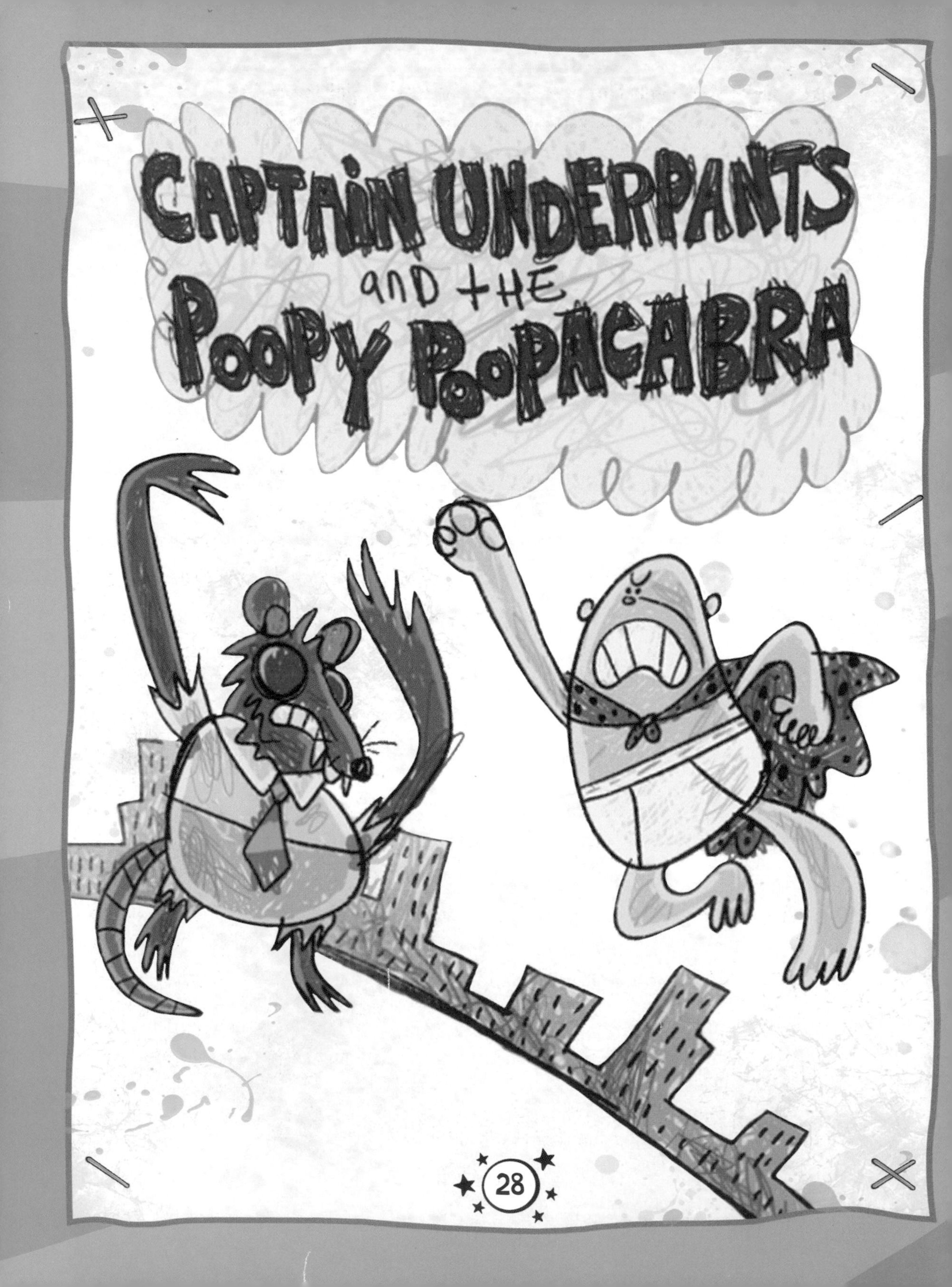
CAPTAIN UNDERPANTS
and the
POOPY POOPACABRA

Once there was this teacher who wanted to get invited to parties. But he didn't, because he smelled like beans because he always made cheesy bean dip that smelled like beans.
ParTAY TiME!
Party
NO BEANS!
EYOO!
That made him all mad and stuff, so he made a sewage sprayer to ruin the parties.
SPLORT!

But when he pressed the button, all the sewage went on him—whoa, wrong way!—and turned him into . . . Poopacabra!
DOUBLE SPLORT
GORT!
FLORT!

AHH!
POOPACABRA!

Poopacabra crashed the party with his stink. Ew!
GORSCH!
LIM-BO! LIM-
But Captain Underpants was there doing the limbo.

Poopacabra made everything stink so bad that Captain Underpants told him they should take it outside.
EXIT
SERIOUSLY. I CAN'T BREATHE.
But Poopacabra punched Captain Underpants through the wall, and it was ON!

VS
Captain Underpants grabbed a lawn gnome and smashed it over Poopacabra's head!
Poopacabra grabbed a pink flamingo and swung it—FLAMINGO!
KONK

And they whacked each other with all the lawn ornaments around. But it was okay, because no one was really going to miss those lawn ornaments. Right?

But right when he was about to chuck a plastic snowman, Captain Underpants saw a single tear in Poopacabra's eye.

And he realized that Poopacabra was just a good guy who had caught a bad and very smelly break.

So, Captain Underpants told everyone to invite Poopacabra to parties.
PoopacaBrA is GOOD!!
IYAM!
HEY! INVITE POOPACABRA TO PARTIES!
And everyone loved Poopacabra's cheesy bean dip because it was made of beans and cheese and what's not to love?
THE END!

CAPTAIN UNDERPANTS
and the
SINISTER SPLOTCH
By Beard and Hutchins
LAWYERS-at-LAW
Attorneys
a

One time, there was an evil robe guy named Splotch. He looked a lot like a certain you-know-who. I'm talking about Captain Underpants!

Splotch wanted to take over the world with robes, which doesn't sound like a great plan, but yeah . . .

So, he pretended to be Captain Underpants but dark and evil, and he started messing stuff up.

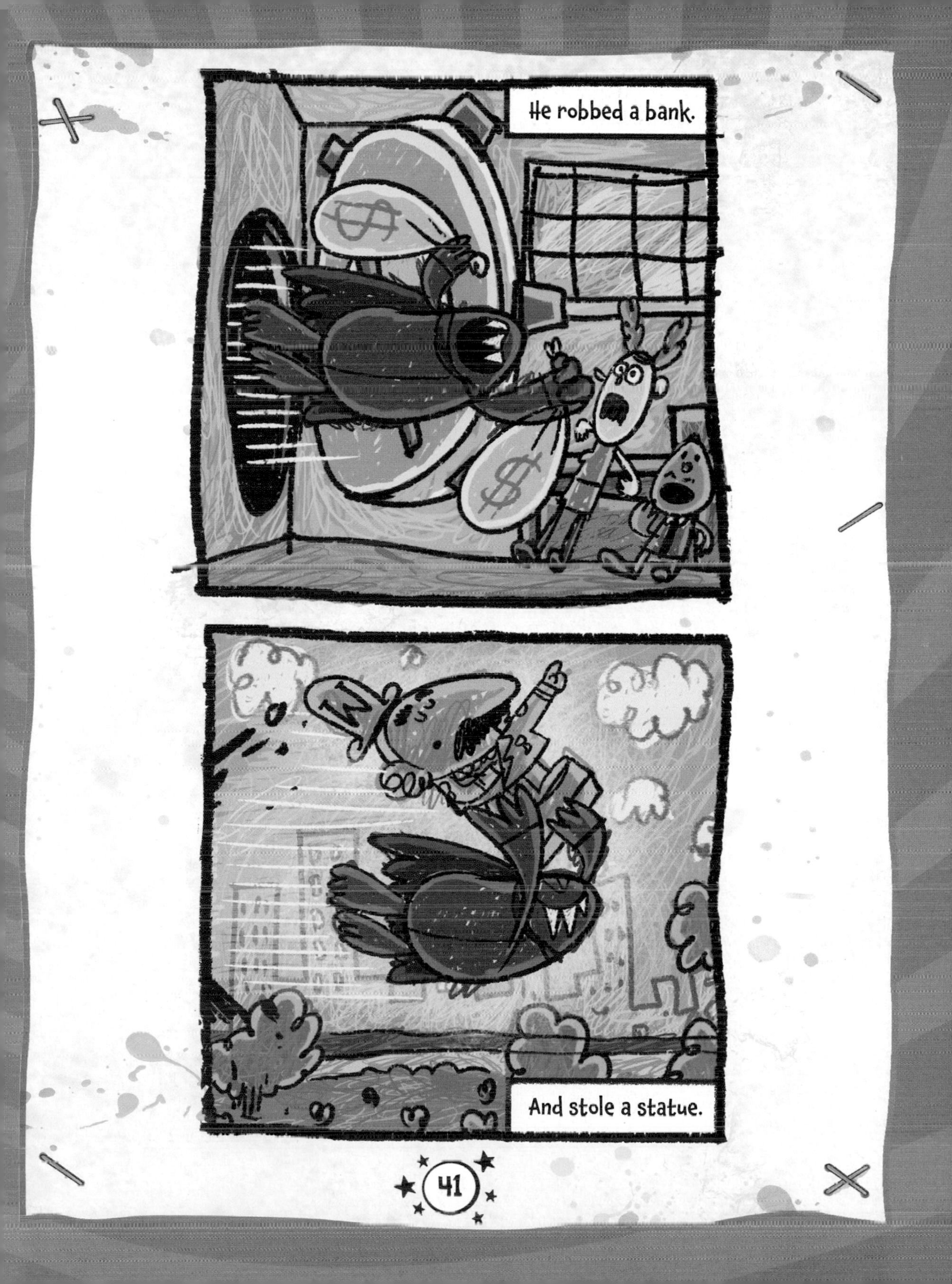
He robbed a bank.
And stole a statue.

And held up traffic.
And put an elephant on a skyscraper.

And set a lake on fire, which is . . . hard.
It was crazy. And the people started blaming Captain Underpants!
CAPTAIN UNDERPANTS, YOU'VE CHANGED, MAN!

The cops put him in jail!
CLANG!
BUT IT WASN'T ME! I WAS HOME MAKING NACHOS!

Splotch's evil plan had worked! Captain Underpants was locked away for good!
YEAH! NOW I'M ON EVIL EASY STREET!
EZ
Next, Splotch made evil dryer sheets—which is, like, a weird laundry thing—that let him control robes.

And he could use the robes to conquer everything. Showers, bouncy houses, taco trucks . . . everything!
Normally, Captain Underpants would show up and be like, "TRA-LA-LAAAAA!" and punch the shady guy who looked like him but shady.
TRA-LA-LAAA!

But not this time, because he was in jail for someone else's crimes, and that someone else was Splotch.

So, in closing, unless you want to get bad stuff happening to everybody, someone should probably let Captain Underpants out of jail.

CAPTAIN UNDERPANTS
And The
SECRET WEAPON
OF THE
STONE-FACED KIDS

One time, there were these serious stone-faced kids who didn't know how to have fun.
MORE MATH, PLEASE.
YES, I'LL VACUUM THE DRIVEWAY, THANK YOU!

One of the stone-faced kids had a birthday party and hired an accountant to write numbers on a chalkboard. Nobody smiled or giggled or said the word *pickle*—at all. I mean, c'mon, *pickle*!

Then these aliens came down and demanded to hear laughter.

SHOW US THE SOUND OF HUMAN LAUGHTER OR WE WILL MESS UP YOUR PLANET!

But since the stone-faced kids didn't know how to have fun, they didn't know how to laugh. They tried cleaning the silverware drawer and ironing a skirt, but it didn't work.

The aliens were going to blast the planet to bits with their blast ray!

But then Captain Underpants came swooping in like Captain Underpants swooping in.
I'LL SAVE EARTH AND JUNK WITH ENTERTAINMENT!
He flew into a haystack and popped up with hay in his ears and said "Pickle!" But the aliens didn't get it.

So, Captain Underpants did all his best basketball tricks: the Fibbidy Floop, the Aqua Duck, and for his big finish, the Diggidy Diggidy Diggidy Doop! That's with nine balls!

The aliens still didn't get it. But the kids had never seen anything so amazing.
They started smiling and their faces cracked and their dumb old frowns fell right off their faces!

The unhappy aliens knocked Captain Underpants far away.
WE WILL BLAST YOUR PLANET AND JUNK. WHAT DO YOU SAY ABOUT THAT?
And the birthday party kid said . . . "Pickle!" And all the kids laughed and laughed really hard for the first time ever!

But it turned out that the sound of laughter was super painful to the aliens, and they covered their one ear.
OW, THAT HUMAN LAUGHING! STOP YOUR NOISING! AH! AH!
And the kids all said, "Pickle! Pickle!! PICKLE!!!"

So, the aliens flew away forever and Captain Underpants flew back in.
TRA-LA-LAAAAA—WHERE'D THEY GO?
The END?

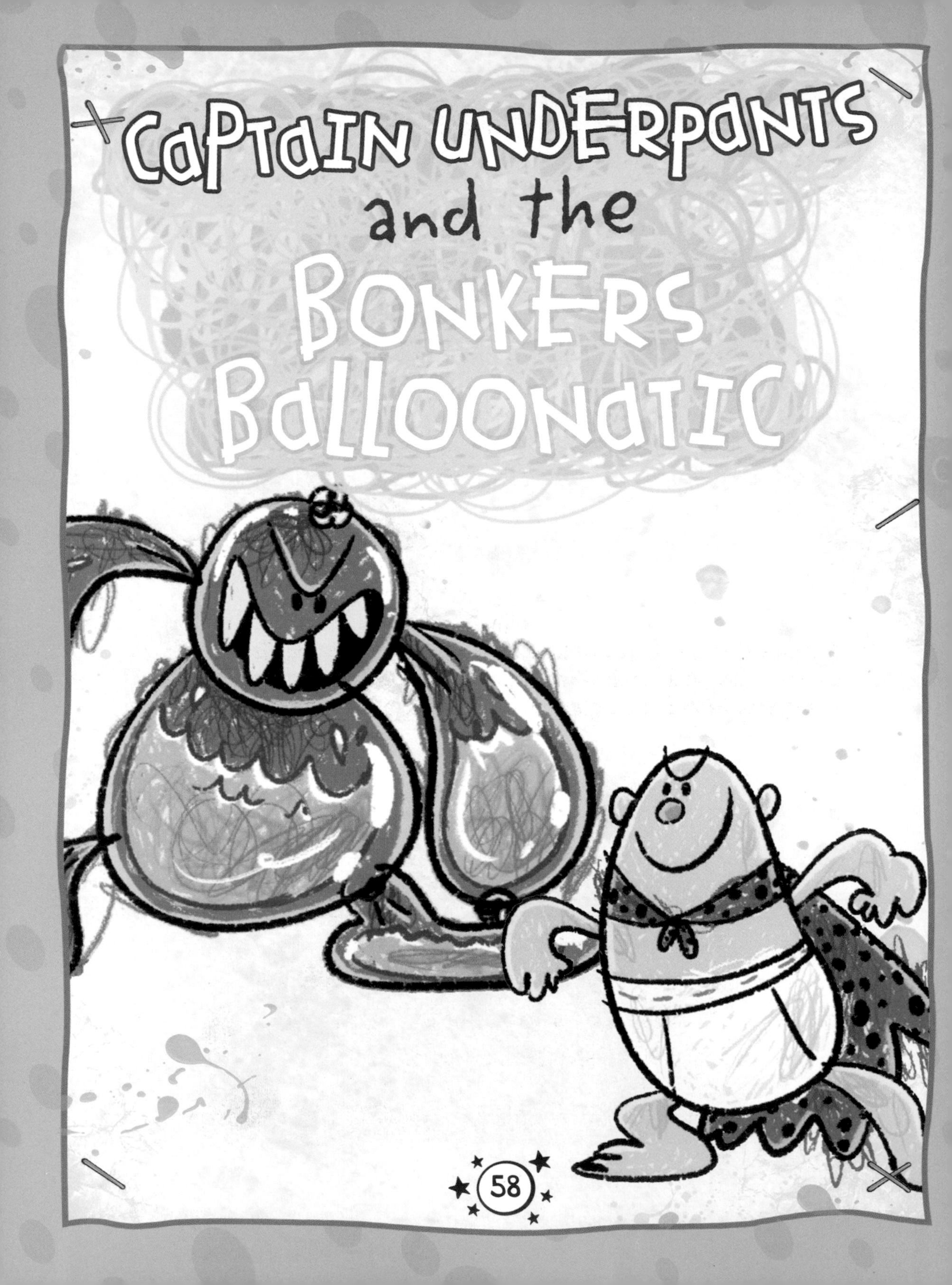
CAPTAIN UNDERPANTS
and the
BONKERS
BALLOONATIC

One time, at camp, it was superhot, and Captain Underpants was drinking a tall, delicious glass of water because, well, WATER.

The kids at camp wanted water, too. But they couldn't find glasses, so, they filled up a bunch of water balloons instead. The balloons got so big they turned into a giant monster named Bonkers Balloonatic!

The campers were still thirsty, so they finally found some glasses and asked Balloonatic for their water back. But he wouldn't let them have any! Even though it was, like, a thousand degrees outside.
SHARING IS FOR THE WEAK!
So, Captain Underpants had to fight Balloonatic! But he wasn't worried. After all, he was no stranger to water.
WATER IS MY JAM!

It was go time! Captain Underpants attacked his rubbery rival with the Skivvy Scuffle.

But Balloonatic repelled him with Elastic Endurance and Crazed Crackle—which was totally cray cray!

HOOHEEHOOHEEHEE!

That gave the Waistband Warrior an idea.
THE ONLY WAY TO BEAT CRAY CRAY IS TO BE CRAY CRAY.
I'VE GOT TO THINK OUTSIDE THE BOX!
BOX

So, he put on a chicken suit and took the Balloonatic bowling, which was pretty far outside the box.

It turned out that Balloonatic was bad at bowling. Like, really bad. So, Captain Underpants had to put his personal feelings aside and show compassion.

He taught the weepy water-hogger to become a world-class professional bowler. And from that day forward, Balloonatic shared both his water AND his love of bowling with the world. Okay, the end.

SURE GLAD I HELD ON TO THIS CHICKEN SUIT— OUTSIDE THE BAAAAAAWKS!

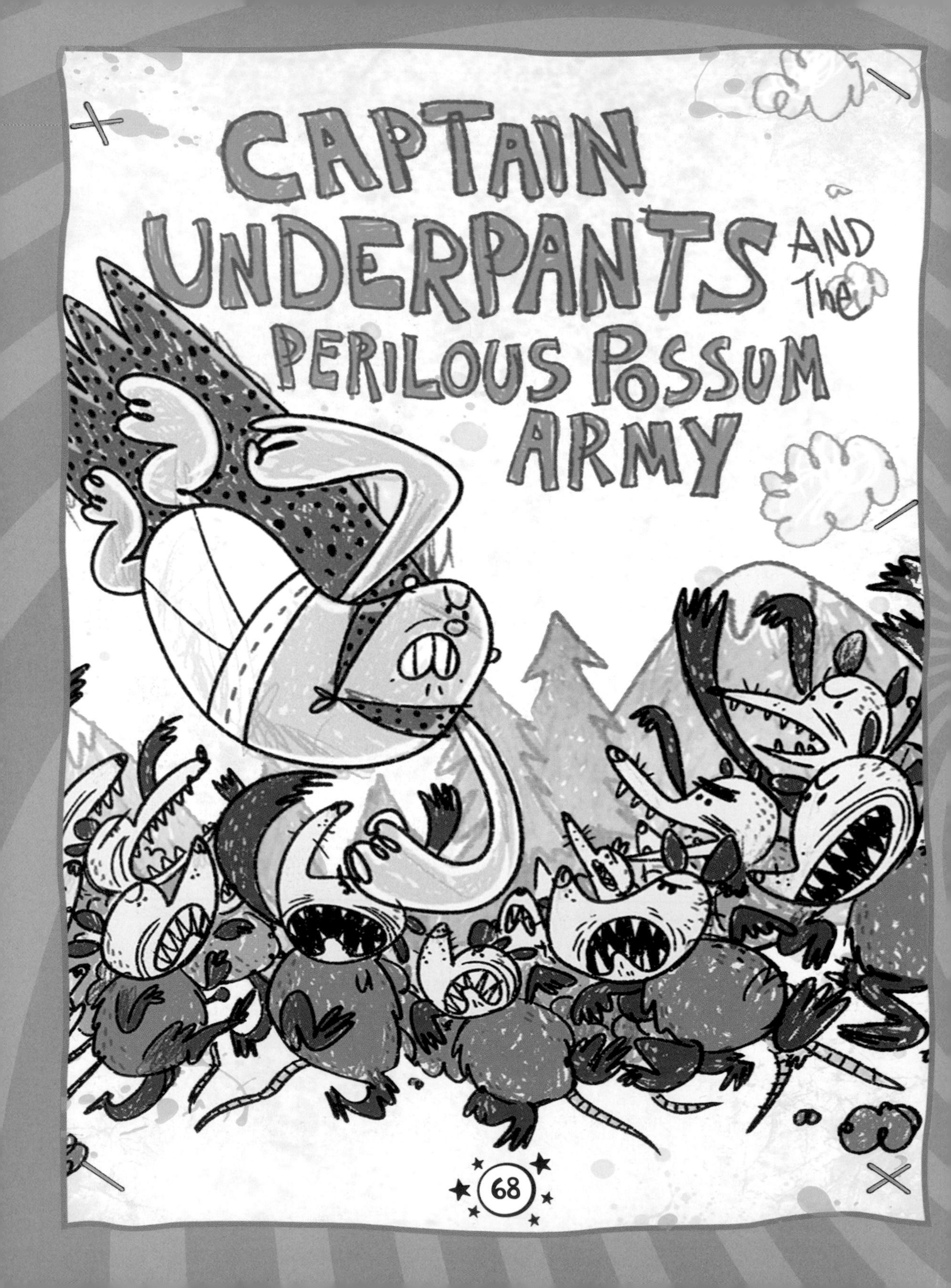
CAPTAIN UNDERPANTS AND THE PERILOUS POSSUM ARMY

A long time ago, there was an evil camp director named Mr. Brupp.

He hated possums, so he chained them up and made them do his bidding. Like make him ricotta french toast and clean the back of his car.

But mostly he used the possums to scare kids at camp so they, like, wouldn't do fun stuff that annoyed him, like play tether-ball with a ham.
YAY! WE LOVE TETHERHAM!
AHHH! HERE COME THE POSSUMS! NOW WE CAN'T PLAY TETHERHAM!
REEE-SHA-ZAI!

Luckily, Captain Underpants was taking a class at a nearby adult school when he heard the noise.
THAT'S THE SOUND OF POSSUMS USING FEAR AS A WEAPON TO KEEP KIDS FROM FUN STUFF LIKE TETHERHAM!
So, he smashed through the wall of the building he was in, even though the door was right there.
OH, YEAH!
KER-SMASH!

But he was deep inside the building, so he had to keep smashing through a bunch of walls in order to get outside.

SMAAAAAA

ASSSSHHHHHH!

Finally, Captain Underpants flew into the camp to save the day!
ZZZZZZZZZZSHRRRRRW!
But there were too many possums for Captain Underpants to fight. So, he decided to trick them by pointing at something and making them look away.
LOOK OUT BEHIND YOU, POSSUMS!

And when they turned around, he smacked them with his Wedgie Whip!
KERSLAP!!
Captain Underpants realized that tricking the possums was too easy.
ADULT SCHOOL
IT'S LIKE THESE POSSUMS NEVER EVEN WENT TO SCHOOL.

So, he brought them all to his adult school building to learn stuff, like camp counseling and bioengineering.
ADULT SCHOOL

The possums got smart and they were so grateful that they never had to scare kids for evil Mr. Brupp ever again.

CAPTAIN UNDERPANTS
and the
ABOMINABLE ALTITOOTH

One time, there was a snow monster with giant teeth named Altitooth. He lived on top of a mountain by himself and howled a lot, like a coyote who lost his job.
WOO-OW-WHACK!
His howls made all the townspeople freak out!
WHOA!
WHAT IS THAT NOISE?
IT SOUNDS LIKE A COYOTE WHO LOST HIS JOB!

So, the mayor called Captain Underpants to get Altitooth to knock it off.
SURE! I'LL BET I CAN TEACH HIM TO YODEL INSTEAD OF HOWL. I'VE BEEN PRACTICING FOR YODELING CLASS!

So, Captain Underpants flew up to the mountain.
TIME TO GET MY YODEL ON!

And he yodeled to show Altitooth how it was done. But it didn't actually sound like yodeling, because Captain Underpants was getting a D+ in his yodeling class.
YO DUG HO LA KO!
That made Altitooth mad. He lashed out like a coyote who can't find a job!
YOU GIVE YODELING A BAD NAME!!

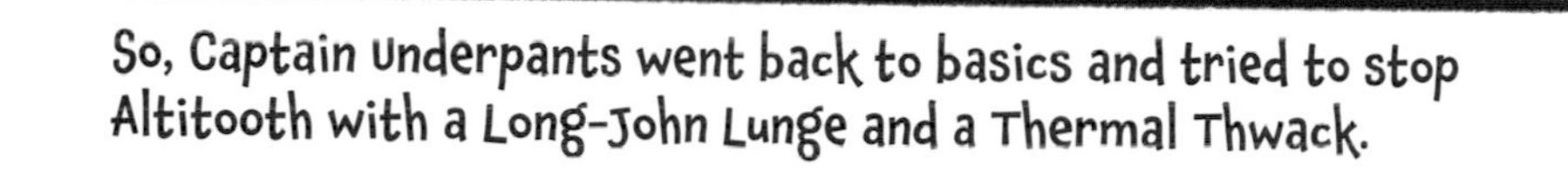
So, Captain Underpants went back to basics and tried to stop Altitooth with a Long-John Lunge and a Thermal Thwack.

THWACKITY-THWACK!

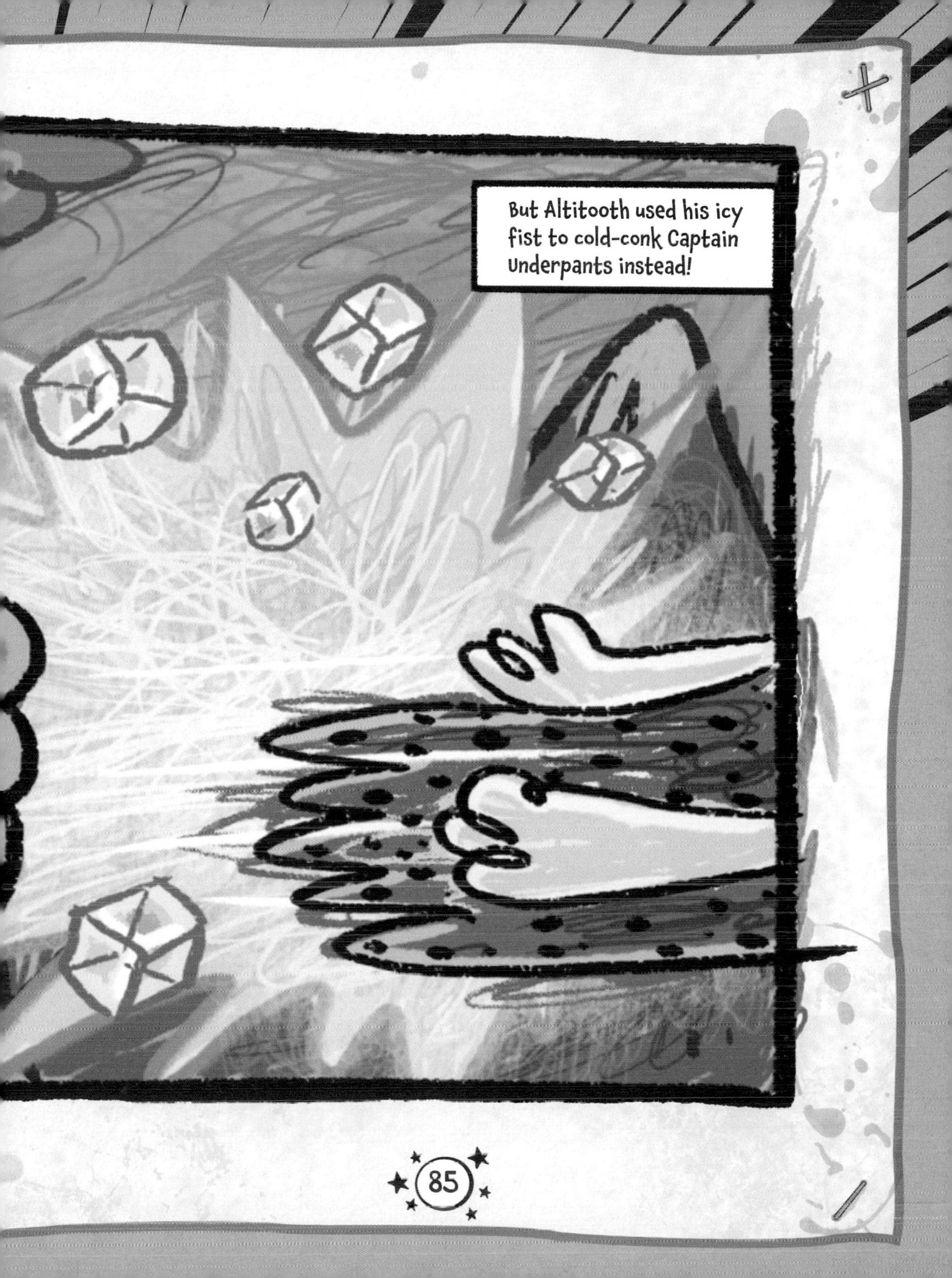
But Altitooth used his icy fist to cold-conk Captain Underpants instead!

Captain Underpants needed another tactic. So, he used an attack yodel to try and knock Altitooth out.
WEEHONOHOSOHO
And what happened then? Altitooth started to cry!
THAT SOUNDS JUST LIKE THE YODEL-BY MY MOMMY USED TO SING TO ME!

That's when Captain Underpants realized the real battle was the one raging between Altitooth and his parents. So, he used all the tools he'd learned at the Healing with Feeling workshop to help Altitooth work through his issues.

And Altitooth made up with his parents and took out a small business loan to open a fondue restaurant. They even hired a coyote as a chef, but that was a huge mistake.

CAPTAIN UNDERPANTS
AND
THE
BEASTLY BARFILISK
by George Beard +
Harold HUTCHINS!

Once, a bunch of kids were on a scavenger hunt, which is like losing the remote and trying to find it under a couch and stuff, but fun.

They had to find an ostrich egg, which is like an ostrich, but not born yet, so it's still an egg.

They went into the woods and found a HUGE egg. A girl named Barbara said it was an ostrich egg.
THAT'S DEFINITELY AN OSTRICH EGG.
But the egg cracked open and a baby chicken-lizard monster crawled out! Now Barbara said it was a Barfilisk egg, because she'll say anything to be right.
90

Then Barbara got bossy.
DON'T LOOK INTO ITS EYES OR YOU'LL BARF A RAINBOW!
But no one listened, and they looked into its eyes anyway. And they all started barfing rainbows! Because even Barbara is right occasionally.

Then the baby Barfilisk's mom showed up, and things were *not* all sunshine and rainbows.
Luckily, Captain Underpants was nearby in the woods looking for his remote.
GORF!
SOUNDS LIKE SOME KIDS ACCIDENTALLY MESSED WITH A BARFILISK EGG! I HAVE GREAT HEARING!

And he flew in to save them. He thought he was immune to the Barfilisk's rainbow barfing powers.
HA! YOU CAN'T MAKE ME BARF!

But he was wrong.
BAAAAAARR

RLOOGA!

Captain Underpants rainbow-barfed with such force that it blasted the Barfilisk's mom into outer space!
But Captain Underpants didn't want to raise the baby Barfilisk on his own—he didn't know the first thing about baby Barfilisks.

So, he flew to outer space and brought the mom back for a Barfilisk family reunion.
And everybody had a blast, except for Barbara, who never enjoys the moment. Okay, the end!

CAPTAIN UNDERPANTS
and the
MASSIVE
MELVIATHAN!

There was once a volcano stunt show called *Magma-nificent* where acrobats did stunts over a live volcano!

It was really cool and totally dangerous.

Captain Underpants was the star because the lava couldn't hurt him.
He was always falling *into* the lava, and that was a big crowd-pleaser!
KERSPLOOSH
HISS
OW
ALOE-VER
Unfortunately, he fell into the lava one too many times and woke up Melviathan, a giant, annoying, multiarmed serpent who lived in the volcano.

OH, NO—
YAY!
WHOOPSIE!

Melviathan didn't like that they were having a stunt show in *his* volcano.

So, he unleashed his Octopunch on Captain Underpants, which is eight punches at once! And he knocked Captain Underpants out.

When Captain Underpants woke up, he was in a secret lab because the President of Earth had saved him.

The lab workers put Captain Underpants through an enhanced-soldier program.

And he turned into **CAPTAIN ULTRAPANTS**! He had lasers, axes, robot-snake arms, surround sound, and a taco bar! So . . . everything!

When his transformation was finally complete, Captain Ultrapants flew back to the volcano with his new foot booster rockets. (He didn't really need them, because he could already fly, but they looked really cool.)

FROOSH
WASACK
Captain Ultrapants unleashed every weapon he had at the same time on Melviathan!

BAPBAPBAP
TACO BAR NOISES!

Melviathan was defeated, both physically and emotionally.
I'M OUT! AND BY THAT I MEAN I'M MOVING!

So, the people had their volcano back. And they turned *Magma-nificent* into a Broadway show, but it lost a lot of its charm.

CAPTAin UNDERPANTS
And the
SLIMY
SALAMANGLER

Once, there was a mean lady with a bad wig that everybody knew was a wig.
This lady was flush happy. Instead of throwing stuff away like a normal person, she flushed it down her toilet like the toilet bowl was a magic portal.
Nothing was safe from her flush-happy ways. Leftovers, old rugs, even hazardous waste!

One time she flushed a salamander because she thought it was gross.
But it turned out her toilet *was* a magic portal!
And it turned the salamander into a monster named Salamangler!
!!!!
ROARRRRR!!!

Salamangler tracked down the flush-happy lady with the bad wig and scared her so much that she put her house on the market, even though it was a bad time to sell.

But Salamangler wanted revenge on *all* the people who'd ever called him disgusting or yucky or not management material. So, he started going down on downtown!
BOOSH
BOOSH
BOOSH!

Luckily, Captain Underpants was on the corner selling gyros because his buddy Dimitri asked him to watch his gyro cart while he was on jury duty.
Just then, Salamangler threw a van on top of the gyro cart!
TRA-LA-LAMB! DIMITRI'S GONNA FLIP!
KERSLANK!

Then, Salamangler tail-slapped Captain Underpants through a bank.
BOOSH!
CLINKLE!
CLINKLE!
COINS!
Since he was already there, Captain Underpants stopped in the bank to try to get a loan to pay for Dimitri's ruined cart. But after he did that, he made a Skivvy Snare and lassoed Salamangler's tail.
KERPAP-WHAP!

But the tail pulled off and Salamangler grew a new one, because that's how salamanders roll.
Captain Underpants was impressed!
WOW! YOU'VE GOT TAIL GAME!
And Salamangler was touched, because that was the nicest thing anyone had ever said to him.

So, he stopped tearing down buildings and started tearing down walls between humans and salamanders by starting SAPI, the Salamander Awareness Program Institute.
S.A.P.I.
THE END
NOTE: No salamanders were hurt in the making of this comic.

CAPTAIN UNDERPANTS
And the
COVERT CAMOFLUSH

One time, this kid Keith had a paintball party for his birthday.
PaintBall
But the kids had to learn paintball safety rules first, and they were super boring!
Rules 101
GROAN!
SNORE!
I'D RATHER BE DOING CHORES!

Captain Underpants was there, too, even though he wasn't invited.
DO I KNOW YOU? YOU'RE AN ADULT.

Once paintball rules were over, Captain Underpants started chowing down on the cake and chugging a gallon of fruit punch.
CHOMP!
H!c!
BUT IT'S NOT TIME FOR CAKE YET!
CHUUUUUUUGGGG!
SLURP.

Then, Captain Underpants started playing paintball. And the kids were loving it!
SHWAP-SHWAP-SHWAP
But suddenly, Captain Underpants had to pee really bad because of that gallon of fruit punch he'd drank.
TRA-LA-LA! GOTTA GO!

APAPAPAP! PAINT!
SHWUP-SHWAP-WAPING!
So, he found a portable potty.

But it turned out the portable potty was actually an alien on vacation. Crazy, right?
Keith called the alien Camoflush because sometimes Keith is a jerk like that.

That made Camoflush really mad, because aliens have feelings too, you know?
So, Camoflush turned invisible.
POOFT!
And he started giving all the kids wedgies because sometimes *he* was a jerk like that, too!

Luckily, Captain Underpants came to the rescue. He loaded up his Skivvy Slingshot with paintballs . . .
FWAH!
SHWAPING
SHWUPOW!
. . . and fired!
The paint went everywhere and made Camoflush visible again.

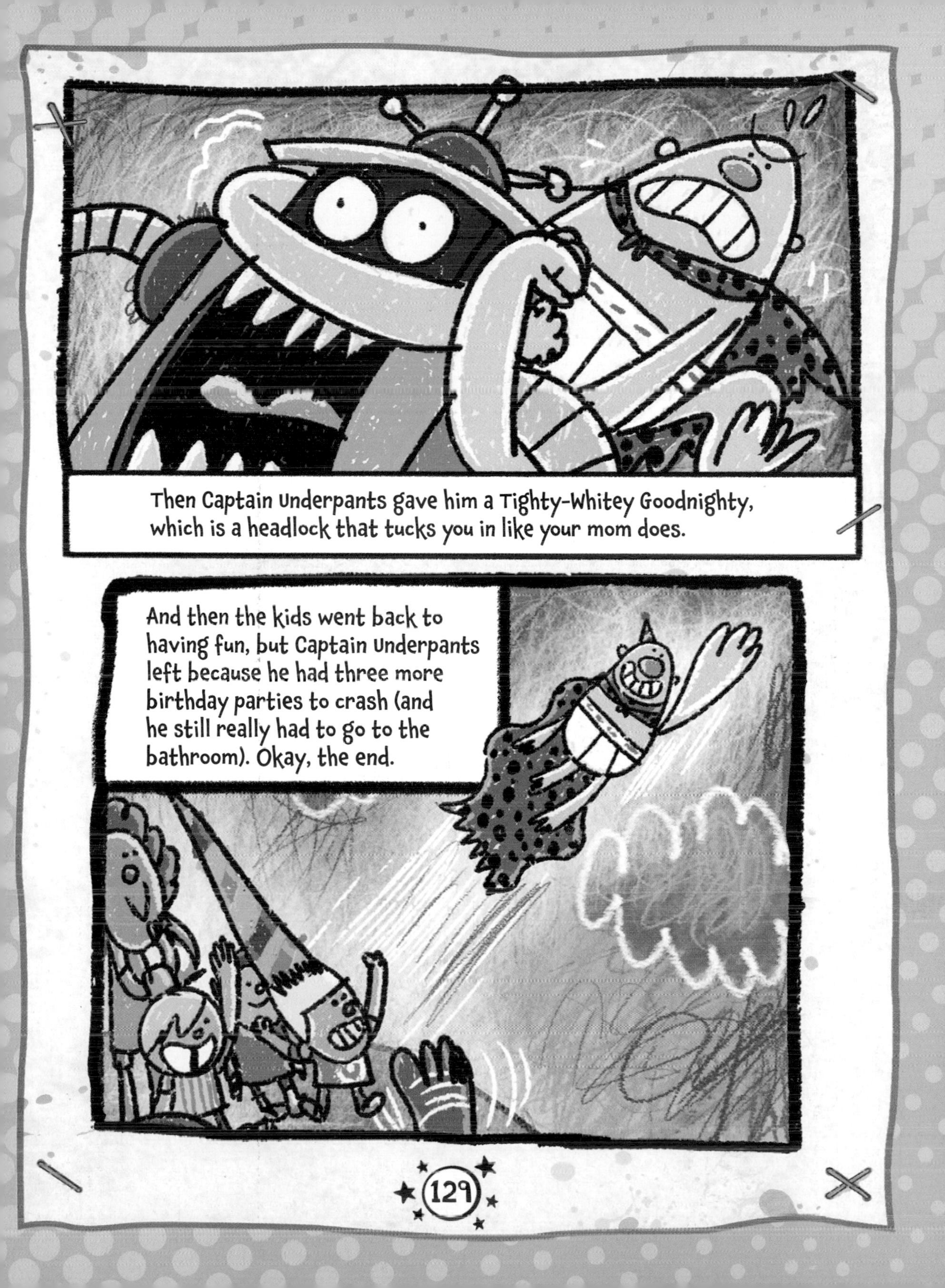
Then Captain Underpants gave him a Tighty-Whitey Goodnighty, which is a headlock that tucks you in like your mom does.
And then the kids went back to having fun, but Captain Underpants left because he had three more birthday parties to crash (and he still really had to go to the bathroom). Okay, the end.

CAPTAIN UNDERPANTS and the BLAH BORELOCK!
BLAH BLAH blah blah BLAH blah BLAH blah BLAH BLAH BLAH blah BLAH blah blah BLAH BLAH BLAH

Once, there was a guy whose stories bored everyone—kids, domestic cattle, paint, even his own parents, Dennis and Celia.

The guy didn't like being boring.

So, he enrolled in Munkchip Night School of Magic Stuff.

He got a certificate in practical sorcery.

And he became Borelock, the Wizard of Dullness!
SNORE
THUNDER NOISE!

Now when he told a boring story, people didn't just fall asleep or pretend to be on the phone. They got bored stiff—for real! Because MAGIC!
NOW THEY HAVE TO LISTEN TO MY STORIES. AND SO WILL THE REST OF THE WORLD!
So, Borelock set out to make the world his captive audience with stories about cleaning his carpet, returning duplicate birthday presents, and shopping for place mats.

Luckily, Captain Underpants was returning a can opener that had a bad attitude.
RETURNS
DO YOU HAVE A RECEIPT?
ONCH!
ONCH!
He saw Borelock turning the other customers into statues with tales of lost luggage.

Even Captain Underpants got bore-alyzed!

But somehow, he was still able to move his tongue.

PFFFTTTT—

So, he made his tongue a lasso and tongue-tied Borelock.
SKLOOSH!

Borelock bawled and bawled. And not just because he was wrapped in Captain Underpants's slobbery tongue.

Captain Underpants realized Borelock just needed a friendly ear to listen to him. So, he volunteered to listen, mainly because he can sleep with his eyes open. And all the people were saved from being bored stiff.

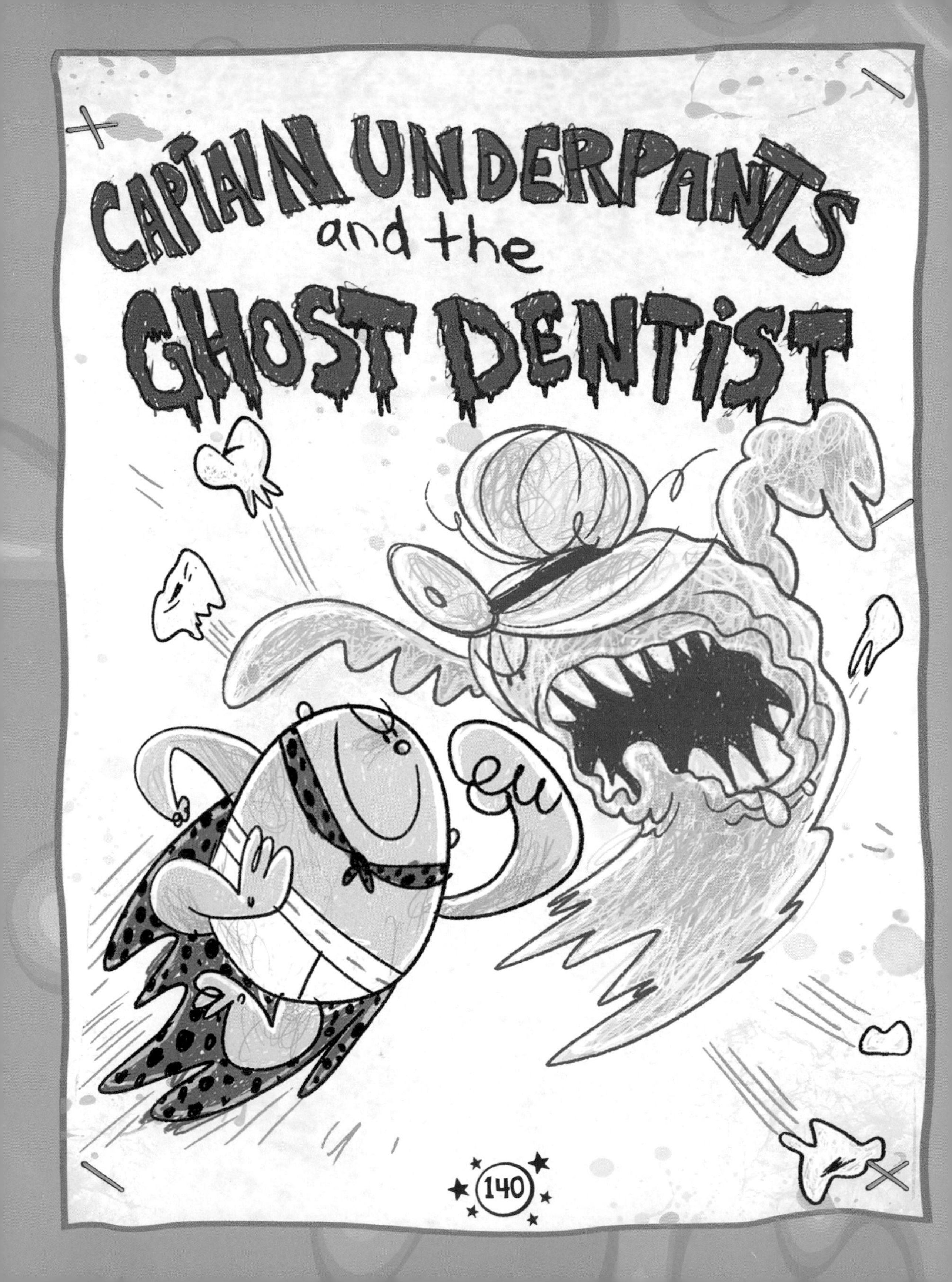
CAPTAIN UNDERPANTS
and the
GHOST DENTIST

Once, there were these ghost experts named Mr. Mupp and Krelvin.
They came to town and warned everyone that Gumbalina Toothington, a giant ghost dentist, was on a rampage.
LOOK OUT! SHE'S A COMIN'!

The ghost experts offered to sell everyone cans of BooBeGone ghost repellent.
ONE SPRAY AND GOODBYE GHOSTY!
ONLY $39.99— FREE GHOST GOGGLES INCLUDED!
But the townspeople didn't believe them.
GHOSTS ARE ONLY REAL IN MOVIES!

But then, Gumbalina Toothington really *did* show up!
WE WERE WRONG!
KA-CHING!
CLANK!
So, the townspeople called the ghost experts back and threw money at them to buy BooBeGone.

They sprayed ghost repellent everywhere. It made everything smell like cinnamon, which was good unless you hate cinnamon.
But Gumbalina came back anyway!
SMELLS GREAT, BUT YOU'RE GOING TO NEED A LOT MORE THAN BOOBEGONE TO GET RID OF ME!

SNIFF
SNIFF
100 MILES!!!
Luckily, Captain Underpants picked up the scent of the cinnamon from a hundred miles away because he has super smell and he LOVES cinnamon buns.
TRA-LA-LICIOUS! WHERE THE BUNS AT?

But when he got to the town, did he find cinnamon buns? No! He found Gumbalina instead!
YOU KNOW THE DRILL, RIGHT? BECAUSE YOUR TEETH ARE ABOUT TO!

Captain Underpants wasn't about to give up that easily, though. He took out his undie-chucks (which are nunchucks made of undies) and twirled them all around the ghost.

WHIR-WHIR!
He knocked Gumbalina down—and she split in half!

The people all thought ghost guts would spill out. But the ghost experts popped out instead!

Because they weren't really ghost experts at all. They were just con men in a ghost costume, and their BooBeGone was just cinnamon-roll scented air freshener.

So, the people sent the con men packing. Then they celebrated not being haunted anymore, and Captain Underpants ate a can of BooBeGone because it still tasted like a cinnamon bun, only crunchy.

The End!

CAPTAIN UNDERPANTS
AND the
CROOKED COMBOTATO!

One day, Captain Underpants went to a party on the roof of a giant skyscraper building.

But when he arrived, the only other person there was Dr. Cons Tuber, a mad scientist who loved potatoes.

WHAT PARTY? DID I GET THE DATE WRONG?
NO, ZIS IS ZE DAY! VECAUSE ZIS IS NOT A PAHTEE—IT IS A TRAP!

Cons Tuber pulled a lever . . .
KER-CHUNK!
. . . and Captain Underpants was buried in mashed potatoes!
I CAN'T MOVE! YOUR SPUDS ARE THICK AS MUD, YO!

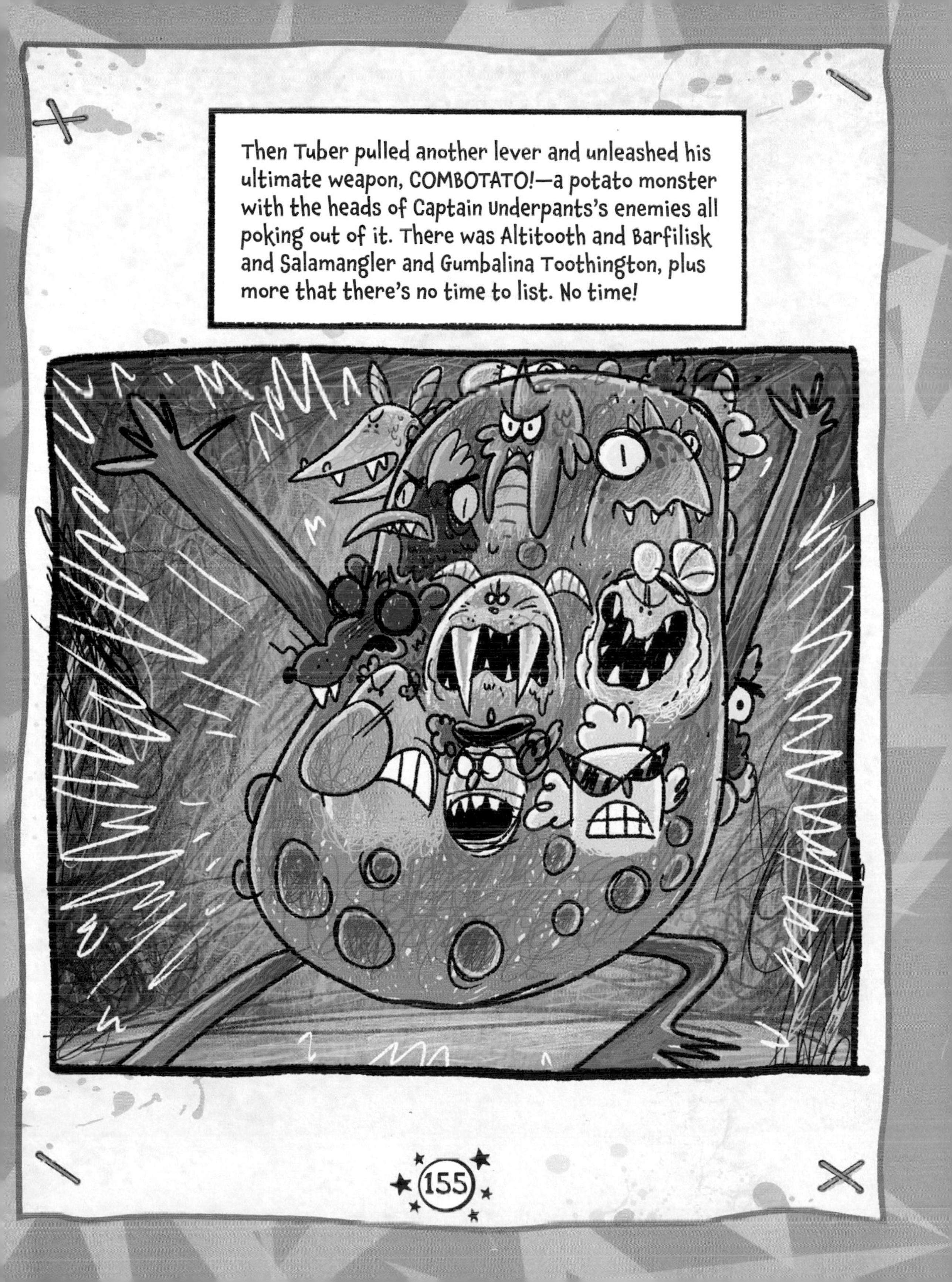
Then Tuber pulled another lever and unleashed his ultimate weapon, COMBOTATO!—a potato monster with the heads of Captain Underpants's enemies all poking out of it. There was Altitooth and Barfilisk and Salamangler and Gumbalina Toothington, plus more that there's no time to list. No time!

And Cons Tuber pulled another lever.

But it was the wrong lever, and it freed Captain Underpants instead!
HA! YOU HAVE TOO MANY LEVERS, YO!

But Captain Underpants wasn't getting out of things that easily. (That would be a boring comic.) So, Combotato tackled Captain Underpants and they both fell off the building.
SERIOUSLY?

But Combotato forgot one important thing: He couldn't fly, and Captain Underpants could. So, Captain Underpants flew away to safety and Combotato smashed into even *more* mashed potatoes on the ground. It was the shortest party-trap ever and the street smelled like potatoes for, like, a week.

The End!

CAPTAIN UNDERPANTS
And the
ReTURN of The
M.I.S.F.A.R.T.S.!

One morning, Captain Underpants called into the Skippy & The Ape Morning Zoo show on the radio.
And he won a free vacation to Notatrap Island!
But the Ape was actually Dr. Disgruntled. He had been slowly building a radio career just to get revenge on Captain Underpants for the whole doom dome thing from another comic.
I'VE GOT YOU NOW!

And Notatrap Island was actually *Trap* Island! What would Captain Underpants do?!
NOT A TRAP
TRAPS

Luckily, a ragtag band of adventurers called the M.I.S.F.A.R.T.S. was there, too, because they had called into the Scooter & The Wombat Morning Circus show and had *also* won a vacation to the same island. Hey, coincidence happens!
But Dr. Disgruntled wasn't worried.
I MADE ENOUGH TRAPS TO GO AROUND!

He attacked them all with the Mind Mine trap,
the Toot Punch trap, and the Nerd on a Wire trap!

But thanks to Thinks's thinking, Thumps's thumping, Winks's winking, Codes's coding, and the rest of the M.I.S.F.A.R.T.S.'s misfarting, the traps didn't stand a chance!
So, Dr. Disgruntled uncorked his ace of traps: Laserlightmare! A monster made of lasers!

Luckily, Codes gave all the M.I.S.F.A.R.T.S. laser pointers because he gets a deal at Nerds on Third. And there was an epic laser battle!

FIZOO-ZOO-ZOO!
SKEW FIZOO!

Captain Underpants and the M.I.S.F.A.R.T.S. defeated the monster. But the lasers destroyed the entire island!

So, Dr. Disgruntled's plan was ruined. And he had to get a job as the sidekick on the Shady & The Skunk Morning Riot show.
THE END!

CAPTAIN UNDERPANTS
AND THE
STAGGERING
SUGAMECHANGER

Once, there was a camp director named Klupp who was super lazy.
Like, putting-a-recliner-chair-thing-in-your-shower-lazy.

Instead of camp activities that took work, he gave the kids stuff they're not supposed to have.
Like chocolate burgers.
Video games.

And bone-snapping trampolines everywhere. Even the ceiling!

Soon, all the kids were crazy-full of sugar and bouncing dangerously all over the trampolines.
SYNCHRONIZED CEILING TRAMPOLINE JUMPING!!!
But they all crashed into each other!
BOOOM!

And they accidentally created Sugamechanger, a half-sugar, half-video game, half-trampoline monster!
1/2
1/2
1/2

Sugamechanger started busting up the camp like he was scoring points for it.
CABIN CARNAGE! DOCK DEVESTATION! MARSHMALLOW MASSACRE!

Luckily, Captain Underpants was patrolling the woods for lost keys because it was Thursday.
And when he saw Sugamechanger, his eyes grew wide.
THAT MONSTER IS MADE OF ALL MY FAVORITE STUFF! WHAT ARE THE ODDS?!

So, he *ate* Sugamechanger's frosting arms.
He played *Laser Headache* on Sugamechanger's screen chest.
KLAO!
KAMIGRAINE

And he bounced on Sugamechanger's trampoline face!
KAWHEE!
KAWHEE!
BOOOOOOING!

Then Sugamechanger exploded! And all the kids who created him just became regular kids again, except they all had really bad tummy aches from the bouncing and the chocolate and the becoming-a-monster thing.

When the parents found out what had happened at camp, they were super angry.
WHERE IS THE CAMP DIRECTOR, WE WOULD LIKE TO KNOW?
But Klupp was taking a shower nap.
So, the parents sent their kids to comic book camp instead. The end.
COMIC BOOK CAMP

CAPTAIN UNDERPANTS
AND THE
TOILETASTICS
VS.
DIAPERADO
AND THE
POOPETRATORS
BY
GEORGE BEARD + HAROLD HUTCHINS

One time, Captain Underpants stopped an evil diaper villain named Diaperado, who was a lunatic in a baby diaper and a cowboy hat.
But Diaperado had a sneaky plan for revenge.
WHAT I NEED TO BEAT CAPTAIN UNDERPANTS IS A TEAM!

So, Diaperado rounded up the best toilet-themed bad guys he could find.

CLOGNETA, THE PIPE PLUGGER
SMARTSY FARTSY, A TALKING FART
CAMOFLUSH, THE CLOAKED COMMANDO
He named his team the Poopetrators!

Captain Underpants caught wind of Diaperado's plan, and he made a toilet team of his own: the Toiletastics!
SERGEANT BOXERS, THE BRO ONE

PLUNGERINA,
THE TOUGH ONE
FARTQUAKE,
THE AWESOME ONE
COLONEL URINAL,
THE GRIZZLED ONE
THE FLUSHER,
THE OTHER AWESOME ONE

And they all went to Trickle Tom's Trickle Town water park, because it has lots of space and free parking.
The mother of all toilet-team-versus-other-toilet-team fights was on!
VS

SPLOOSH!
WHOSE LEG AM I GRABBING?
KERSWACK!
SHOULD WE TAKE A LUNCH BREAK?
KERPLUNK!
KERBLAMO!

The fight took a turn when the Giggle Gulch slide made the Poopetrators throw up everywhere.

So, they surrendered, and the Toiletastics won. Because good always triumphs over evil—even when it's smelly.
The End!